Also by Nick Butterworth:

One Snowy Night

One Blowy Night

The Rescue Party

With Mick Inkpen:

The Nativity Play

Nice or Nasty

Just Like Jasper

First U.S. Edition
ISBN 0-316-11914-8
Library of Congress Catalog Card Number 94-75958
10 9 8 7 6 5 4 3 2 1
Published simultaneously in Canada by
Little, Brown & Company (Canada) Limited
Printed and bound in China

THE SECRET PATH

NICK BUTTERWORTH

LITTLE, BROWN AND COMPANY
BOSTON NEW YORK TORONTO LONDON

In leafy green hedges,
    the doorway was wide.
You looked and you wondered
    and then stepped inside.
The puzzling pathways
    took you along,
A turn to the right
    turned out to be wrong.
But when all that seemed left
    turned out to be right,
You entered the center,
    a wonderful sight!
But now comes the hard part,
    to find the right track,
To retrace your steps,
    the secret path back.
The maze is a trickster,
    of that there's no doubt.
The maze let you in,
    but it won't let you out!

"I know. It's a shame," said Percy the park keeper to his small friend.

Percy had been looking after a young squirrel who had fallen out of a tree and hurt his arm.

"And I bumped my nose on Thursday," the squirrel went on.

"Mmm, I see," said Percy, who was not really giving the squirrel his full attention.

Percy was busy searching for something.

"Aha! Here it is," said Percy. "String. We'll need this today."

As Percy and the squirrel trundled their way across the park, they didn't notice a group of friends hiding behind a large tree.

"I've been meaning to fix up the old maze for ages," said Percy. "The hedges are terribly overgrown."

"Percy's going to work on the maze," said the fox.

"Let's race him there and have some fun!" said the badger, and he began to whisper excitedly.

The others squeaked with delight as they listened. Only the hedgehog wasn't so sure. He found the maze rather confusing.

"I don't think I'll come," he said.

"I've . . . er . . . got something to do."

Percy parked his wheelbarrow by the entrance to the maze.

"Aren't you worried about getting lost in the maze?" the squirrel asked.

"That's why I need the string," said Percy. "I leave a trail of string from where I'm working back to the entrance of the maze. That way, I can't get lost, you see?"

The squirrel didn't really see because he wasn't really listening.

"I'm not sure whether I like spring or autumn the best," he said.

At the back of the maze, a line of animals was disappearing one by one into the thick hedge.

"We'll go right to the middle and wait for Percy," whispered the badger.

"Then we'll jump out and give him a big surprise," giggled the rabbits.

"Ssshh!" said the fox loudly, which made them all giggle again.

Percy worked hard with his hedge
clippers, and little by little the maze
began to look much tidier. All the time,
Percy followed his string in and out of the
maze.

By now, the surprise party had made its way to the center of the maze, where there stood a stone bench. The bench had been carved to look like a lion.

At first the animals waited eagerly for Percy to come. But Percy took longer than they expected. Soon they began to yawn. Then they fell asleep.

Percy's hedge clippers clacked on and on, only stopping now and then when Percy went to dump a wheelbarrow load of clippings.

As Percy pushed his empty wheelbarrow back toward the maze, a hedgehog called to him.

"Hello Percy. Did you get a big surprise from the animals in the maze?"

"A big surprise?" Percy stopped and smiled. "Er . . . not yet," he said.

When at last Percy and the squirrel worked their way to the center of the maze, there was no big surprise waiting for them.

Percy chuckled at the sight of the sleeping animals in front of him.

"Let's have some fun ourselves," he whispered.

Percy tiptoed to the back of the lion-shaped bench and coughed loudly.

"Ahem. I beg your pardon," said Percy in a deep, growly voice.

The fox opened one eye.

"It's not that I mind so very much," went on
    Percy, "but I do like people to ask before
they go to sleep on me."
    The other animals began to stir.
    The fox stared at the lion's head.
He couldn't believe
his ears.

"I'm very sorry," said the fox. "We didn't realize. We thought you were just a seat." The other animals opened their eyes in amazement to hear the fox talking to a lump of stone. They were even more amazed when the stone answered back.

"Did you indeed?" said the growly voice.

"Just a seat. Hmm."

"We're very sorry," said the fox. "Will you tell us your name?"

Percy growled. "My name is . . . "

But at that moment, one of the rabbits looked behind the bench.

"His name is Percy!" cried the rabbit.

The game was up, and a chuckling Percy came out from behind the bench.

"Percy's tricked *us* instead!" said the badger.

The fox suddenly started to giggle. That got everybody else giggling again.

"Come on," said Percy, as he collected his tools, "who'd like some homemade cookies? I'll show you the way out of the maze. All we have to do is follow my str—"

But Percy didn't finish. Standing there in front of him was his little squirrel helper. The squirrel was holding a large ball of string.

"Don't forget this, Percy," he said. "I've wound it all up for you."

Percy looked dismayed.

"Don't worry," said the fox, "I think this is the way out."

"No, no," said the badger. "I'm sure it's this way."

"Surely it's this way," said another voice.

"I might be wrong," said the squirrel, holding the ball of string, "but I've got a feeling it's this way." Percy groaned.

"And I've got a feeling we'll be having those cookies for breakfast!"